DO NOT TAKE

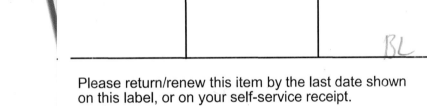

WRITTEN BY JULIE GASSMAN   ILLUSTRATED BY ANDY ELKERTON

On the last day of school, you smile when you wake.
It's been a great year, but you need a break.

You want the day to be totally **fantastic**,
so please avoid doing anything drastic . . .

When the school gathers to celebrate the year,
your dragon will lose control as he cheers.

If you get an award, he won't hide his delight.
He'll flap his wings and take off in **flight!**

Back in the classroom, your desk is a mess.
It's a situation that you must address.

But all the dust will make dragon wheeze.
And then he'll let out a terrible **sneeze!**

SO DO **NOT** TAKE YOUR DRAGON TO THE LAST DAY OF SCHOOL!

It's a class picnic. You can't wait for **lunch!**
Then dragon sits down with a thunderous **crunch!**

He'll squash your friends. He'll steal their dessert.
He'll even eat food that's been dropped in the dirt!

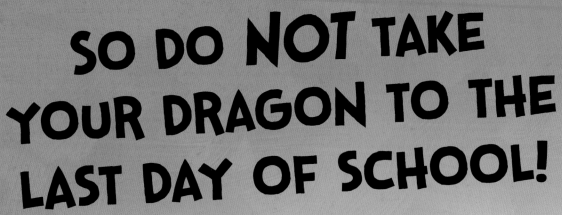

SO DO NOT TAKE YOUR DRAGON TO THE LAST DAY OF SCHOOL!

Dragon should not be playing sports day games.
He pulls too hard and melts hoops with his flames.

And when it's time to compete in the three-legged race,
He'll trip up the competition . . . what a **disgrace!**

But teacher, I want to show him what makes school so great.
The lunch hall, the playground, the art and crafts space!

And I want to show him how you make lessons so fun.
How clever you are – you've taught us a tonne!

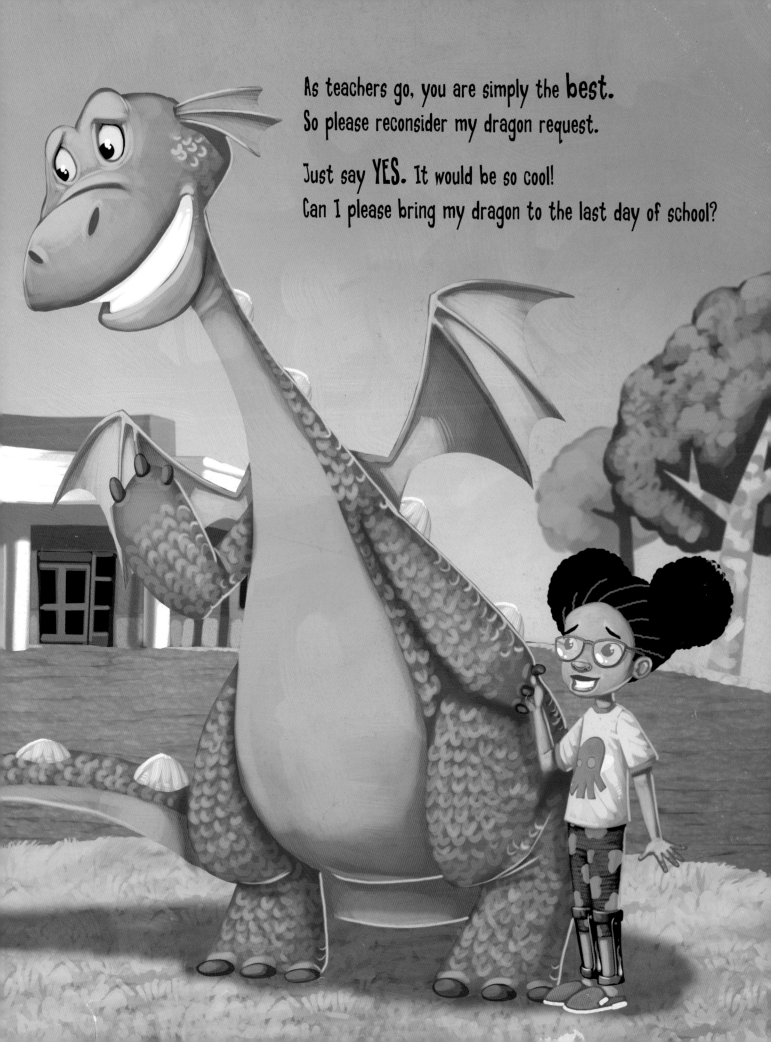

As teachers go, you are simply the **best**.
So please reconsider my dragon request.

Just say **YES**. It would be so cool!
Can I please bring my dragon to the last day of school?

Well, it's been a fun year, but I want the class to myself.
I don't want to share the day with anyone else.

But perhaps he could come at the end of the day
and even join in the last game that we play.

Thank you!
And if saying goodbye is hard, he'll put you at ease
with a big dragon smile and a sweet, loving **squeeze.**

A dragon hug is a wonderful tool . . .

ABOUT THE AUTHOR

The youngest in a family of nine children, Julie Gassman grew up in Howard, South Dakota, USA. After college, she swapped small-town life for the world of magazine publishing in New York City. She now lives in southern Minnesota with her husband and their three children. On the last day of school, Julie and her dragon enjoy having water balloon fights and going out for ice cream.

ABOUT THE ILLUSTRATOR

After 14 years as a graphic designer, Andy decided to go back to his illustrative roots as a children's book illustrator. Since 2002 he has produced work for picture books, educational books, advertising and toy design. Andy has worked for clients all over the world. He currently lives on the west coast of Scotland with his wife and three children.

Raintree is an imprint of Capstone Global Library Limited, a company incorporated in England and Wales having its registered office at 264 Banbury Road, Oxford, OX2 7DY – Registered company number: 6695582

www.raintree.co.uk
myorders@raintree.co.uk

Text and illustrations © Capstone Global Library Limited 2021
The moral rights of the proprietor have been asserted.

Designed by Nathan Gassman

ISBN 978 1 4747 9316 2 (paperback)

British Library Cataloguing in Publication Data
A full catalogue record for this book is available from the British Library.

Printed and bound in India